The Invisible Guest in
MOOMINVALLEY

This book belongs to:

....

Dear Reader,

The book that you hold in your hands is going to whisk you away on an amazing adventure with Moomintroll, his family and their friends in Moominvalley. This story is based on books written by my aunt Tove Jansson almost 75 years ago – books that your parents and their parents might even have read!

As a child I used to love listening to stories read aloud by grown-ups. What a wonderful feeling it was to sit curled up in the crook of someone's arm, listening to the story, looking at the pictures, and seeing new pictures drawn in my mind. It was my favourite part of the day, and it made me the book lover that I still am. I hope that these books will inspire the same feeling in you – we're off on an adventure to the magical world of Moominvalley, where absolutely anything can happen!

Sophia Jansson,

Tove Jansson's niece and Creative Director of Moomin Characters

Tove Jansson and some of the inhabitants of Moominvalley

The Invisible Guest in MOOMINVALLEY

Adapted from the *Tove Jansson* classic

CECILIA DAVIDSSON • FILIPPA WIDLUND

MACMILLAN CHILDREN'S BOOKS

Some of Moominvalley's inhabitants

Moomintroll is curious and friendly. He loves going on adventures, especially if it means spending time with his friends. If ever the adventure becomes too scary, he always has his Moominmamma to come back to.

Moominmamma is soft in all the right places and has a handbag full of dry woolly socks, stomach powder and sweeties. She never loses her cool, and makes sure that every little creature in Moominvalley has a place to sleep if they need it.

Moominpappa is a very well-travelled fellow, at least according to him. He often longs for wild adventures like the ones he experienced in his youth. Then he sits in his room and writes his memoirs, a long book about his great escapades.

Little My is very little, as her name suggests. In fact she is so little that she can hide in Moominmamma's work basket. Little My knows no fear, and when confronted by danger she reacts in the same way as she does when confronted by people in general: by biting.

Too-ticky is a friend of the Moomin family and likes to stay in their bathhouse. She is a calm person and has practical solutions to most problems. She has the unusual quality of never feeling the need to pander to anybody.

Snorkmaiden loves everything that is beautiful, just like her. She is smart and inventive, but wishes that life in Moominvalley could be more grand and dramatic.

Ninny was never seen or heard much until she came to Moominvalley and met the Moomin family. If you would like to know the story of how that happened, you might want to read this book.

One dark and rainy evening the Moomin
family were sitting around the big table
cleaning mushrooms.

"Little My has picked milkcaps again,"
said Moominpappa, holding up a reddish mushroom.
"Last year she picked fly agaric."

"Let's hope she picks some nice chanterelles next
year," said Moominmamma.

"We live in hope!" laughed Little My.

And they carried on cleaning in contented silence.

Suddenly there came a knock on the door. It was
Too-ticky, who stayed in the family's bathhouse sometimes.
She stepped inside, without waiting for an answer, and
shook the water from her raincoat.

"I've brought a guest," she said, holding the door
open and beckoning out into the rain. "Come on then!"

But no one came.

"Well, if she's too shy to come inside she'll just have to stay out there," said Too-ticky – and she shut the door.

"Who is it?" asked Moomintroll.

"Her name is Ninny," said Too-ticky.

"Isn't she getting awfully wet out in the rain?" asked Moominmamma.

"I don't know if it matters all that much when you're invisible," said Too-ticky.

The family stopped cleaning and waited for an explanation.

"You do know that people can turn invisible if they are frightened too often, don't you?" said Too-ticky, gobbling up a puffball mushroom that looked like a lovely little tuft of snow.

"Well, Ninny here was terribly frightened by a lady who took care of her without really liking her much. I met the lady and she was ghastly. Not angry – you can forgive a little anger sometimes. No, this lady was ice cold. The poor child began to fade away until eventually she became invisible. She disappeared completely last Friday. The lady was ever so cross about it and gave her to me. She said she certainly wasn't going to take care of relatives she couldn't even see."

"So what did you do to the lady? Did you bite her?" said Little My.

"No, violence doesn't help. But I took Ninny and brought her here, so that you can help her become visible again," said Too-ticky.

Everybody around the table was silent for a moment.
The only sound was the rain pattering on the roof.
They were all thinking about what Too-ticky had said.

"Does she speak?" said Moominpappa at last.

"No, but the lady tied a bell around her neck so you
know where she is."

Too-ticky got up and opened the door again.

"Ninny!" she called into the darkness.

The cold scent of autumn streamed in over the verandah.

Soon they heard a ringing outside. It was a cautious,
hesitant ring. The sound came up the steps and then
stopped. A little bell on a band hung in mid-air.

"This is your new family, Ninny. They can be a little
silly at times but they're a decent bunch on the whole,"
said Too-ticky.

The family stared at the hovering bell.

"Give the child a seat," Moominpappa said at last. "Does she know how to clean mushrooms?"

At first the bell stayed completely still. Then something wondrous happened: one of the chanterelle mushrooms started floating through the air!

Yes, the invisible child certainly did know how to clean mushrooms.

Everybody sat quietly and looked on as soil and pine needles were peeled off by invisible paws. The mushroom was sliced into small pieces which then flew into the pan.

"How exciting!" said Little My. "Try giving her something to eat. I wonder if we'll see the food going down into her belly."

"Any idea how we can make her visible again?" asked Moominpappa worriedly. "Perhaps we should take her to the doctor?"

"I don't think so," said Moominmamma. "Maybe she wants to be invisible for a while. I think we ought to leave her in peace until we come up with a plan."

So that's exactly what they did.

Moominmamma went to make up a bed for their invisible guest in the eastern attic room, which happened to be empty. The tinkling bell followed her up the stairs.

Moominmamma lit a candle.

"Now it's Ninny's bedtime. And if you get scared or want anything, just come downstairs and ring your bell." Moominmamma saw the bed covers lift up and form a little mound.

Moominmamma went down to her room and dug
out Granny Moomin's old notebook filled with
home remedies.

She flicked through: *The Evil Eye . . . Cures for
Melancholy . . . The Common Cold . . .* no, thought
Moominmamma.

Eventually she found a note that Granny had scribbled
down in shaky handwriting: *If someone should fade away
and become difficult to see.*

Moominmamma read through the recipe, which
was quite complicated. Then she set about mixing up
the home remedy for little Ninny.

The next morning Moomintroll heard the bell
coming down the stairs. He had been waiting all
morning for their new guest to emerge. But the sight
of the bell was nowhere near as exciting as . . . the paws!
Down they came, hopping from step to step: tiny little
feet with timid little toes all tightly pressed together.
That was all that could be seen of Ninny and it looked
very strange indeed.

Moomintroll rushed out into the garden.
"Moominmamma!" he called. "She's got paws!"

"I thought as much," said Moominmamma up in the apple tree. Granny knew a thing or two, she thought. It was rather cunning of me to mix the home remedy in with Ninny's coffee.

"Splendid," said Moominpappa. "But it'll be better when we can see her snout. I find it rather depressing talking to someone I can't see."

"Shh," Moominmamma warned.
There were Ninny's paws, standing in the grass among the fallen apples.

"Hey, Ninny," yelled Little My. "When are you going to show us your snout? You must look a fright if you want to stay invisible."

"Hush," whispered Moomintroll, "you'll make her sad."

He walked over to Ninny. "Don't worry about Little My. She's a tough one. You're perfectly safe here with us. And don't even think about that terrible lady . . ."

In that very moment Ninny's paws began to fade until they were barely visible in the grass.

"Darling, that wasn't a very nice thing to say," said Moominmamma firmly. "She doesn't want to be reminded about all that. Now pick apples and be quiet!"

Moominpappa brought out a large apple grinder and
they started to make apple jam. Moomintroll turned the
crank while Moominmamma filled it with apples, and
Moominpappa and Ninny, whose paws had become visible
again, carried the filled jars over to the verandah. Little My
sat up in the tree singing 'The Big Apple Song'.

Then suddenly they heard a crash!

In the middle of the gravel path there was a big
splodge of jam surrounded by spiky shards of glass.
And next to the jam, Ninny's paws quickly faded
and disappeared.

"Never mind," said Moominmamma. "That was the
jar we usually give to the bumblebees. Now we don't have
to carry it all the way to the meadow."

Ninny's paws reappeared along with a pair of spindly
legs! Above the legs, the edge of a muddy brown dress
was just about visible.

"I can see her legs!" cried Moomintroll.

"Congratulations," said Little My, looking down from the apple tree. "Though why you'd wear a brown dress is beyond me."

Moominmamma smiled and thought about clever Granny Moomin and her home remedies.

Ninny followed them around all day. They got so used to hearing the tinkling bell that it no longer seemed strange.

Evening came. When all the little ones had gone to bed, Moominmamma found an old rosy-red shawl and sewed it into a little dress. When it was ready she carried it up to Ninny's room and laid it out on a chair. Then she sewed a wide hairband out of the leftover fabric.

The next day Ninny came down for her morning coffee wearing the dress. She curtsied politely when she was given her coffee cup.

"Thank you very much," she squeaked.

The family were stunned. Little My laughed out loud and banged her spoon on the table.

"Great, you've started talking! Let's hope you've got something worth saying. Do you know any good games?"

"No," squeaked Ninny. "But I have heard of games."

"Oh dear," thought Moomintroll. He decided to teach Ninny all the games he knew.

After coffee they went down to the river to play.

But Ninny didn't know how. She curtsied and said "how fun", but the others had a strong suspicion that she wasn't enjoying herself at all. She didn't even try to run away when Moomintroll started chasing her. She just politely let herself be caught.

"You're supposed to run!" bellowed Little My. "Don't you even know how to run and jump?"

Ninny's skinny legs ran and jumped, just as she was told. But soon she came to a standstill with her arms hanging limply by her side.

"What are you waiting for?" cried Little My. "Where's your fighting spirit? Do you want me to punch you on the nose?"

"I'd rather you didn't," said Ninny.

"She has no idea how to play," Moomintroll mumbled. "It's so sad!"

"She doesn't know how to get angry either," said Little My. "That's no good at all. Do you hear me?" She went right up close to Ninny and gave her a menacing look. "You'll never get your face back if you don't learn to stand up for yourself!"

"You're right," Ninny agreed and backed away timidly.

Days passed and nothing changed. Eventually they stopped trying to teach Ninny how to play. She didn't like funny stories either. She never laughed in the right places.

They got used to seeing her rosy-red dress traipsing behind Moominmamma, right up close.

As soon as Moominmamma stopped, the bell stopped ringing too.

When she continued walking, it started again.

Moominmamma continued feeding Ninny Granny's home remedy, but it didn't help.

I suppose people have managed fine without a head before, she thought. And she gave up on the home remedy.

One day the whole family went to the beach to pull their boat ashore before winter. It was a beautiful autumn morning – a little cold around the snout but almost summery in the sunshine. A shower of rain had left everything wet, bright and glistening. Ninny's bell was ringing behind them as usual, but when they came to the sea she stopped dead. Then she lay on her tummy in the sand and started to whimper.

"What's the matter with Ninny? Is she frightened of something?" asked Moominpappa.

Moominmamma bent down and whispered to Ninny. Then she got up and said: "It's the first time she's seen the sea. She thinks it's too big."

"What a silly girl!" muttered Little My.

Moominmamma looked at her sternly and said: "Look who's talking. Now let's pull up the boat."

Once the boat was on land with its keel to the sky, Moominmamma sat on the pier and gazed down into the water.

"Hoo, that looks cold," she said.

Then she yawned and said it had been a long time since anything exciting had happened.

Moominpappa winked secretively at Moomintroll.

He put on a mischievous smile and started sneaking up behind Moominmamma.

Of course Moominpappa wasn't really going to push Moominmamma into the water. He just wanted to joke around with the children.

But before he could reach her they heard a great big yelp and saw a red flash fly across the pier. Moominpappa shrieked and dropped his hat in the water. Ninny had bitten Moominpappa's tail with her invisible teeth — and they were sharp.

"Bravo!" cried Little My. "Couldn't have done it better myself!"

Ninny was standing on the pier with an angry face staring out from beneath a scraggly fringe. She hissed at Moominpappa like an angry cat.

"Don't you dare throw her into the big terrible sea!"

"She's visible, she's visible!" cried Moomintroll. "And she's lovely!"

"I beg to differ," said Moominpappa, eyeing his bitten tail. "That is the meanest, naughtiest child I have ever seen, with or without a head."

Moominpappa lay down on the pier and tried to fish out his hat with his cane. Somehow he managed to slip and fall in head first. He stood on the bottom with his ears full of sludge.

"Oh!" cried Ninny. "How funny! How wonderful!" And she laughed so hard that the whole pier shook.

"That child is even worse than Little My," groaned Moominpappa. "But she's visible, that's the main thing."

"And it's all thanks to Granny," said Moominmamma.

First published 2019 by Bonnier Carlsen Bokförlag, Stockholm
This edition published 2021 by Macmillan Children's Books
an imprint of Pan Macmillan
The Smithson, 6 Briset Street, London, EC1M 5NR
EU representative: Macmillan Publishers Ireland Limited,
Mallard Lodge, Lansdowne Village, Dublin 4
Associated companies throughout the world
www.panmacmillan.com

ISBN: 978-1-5290-1493-8

© Moomin Characters ™
Based on the short story *The Invisible Child*
from *Tales from Moominvalley* by Tove Jansson.

Written by Cecilia Davidsson
Illustrated by Filippa Widlund
Translated by A. A. Prime

1 3 5 7 9 8 6 4 2

A CIP catalogue record for this book is available from the British Library.

Printed in China